THE SNOOPY SHOW

SNOOPY
ON THE JOB

by Charles M. Schulz
Based on *The Snoopy Show* episode "Snoopy on the Job"
written by Carly DeNure
Adapted by Patty Michaels

Ready-to-Read

Simon Spotlight
New York   London   Toronto   Sydney   New Delhi

SIMON SPOTLIGHT

An imprint of Simon & Schuster Children's Publishing Division

1230 Avenue of the Americas, New York, New York 10020

This Simon Spotlight edition December 2021

Peanuts and all related titles, logos, and characters are trademarks of Peanuts
Worldwide LLC © 2021 Peanuts Worldwide LLC.

Manufactured in the United States of America 1121 LAK

10 9 8 7 6 5 4 3 2 1

ISBN 978-1-5344-9888-4 (hc)

ISBN 978-1-5344-9887-7 (pbk)

ISBN 978-1-5344-9889-1 (ebook)

It was a sunny day,
and Lucy was very excited.
She was having a yard sale!

"Step right up!" she shouted.
"Quality merchandise
at reasonable prices!"

"And remember," Lucy continued, "you break it, you bought it!"

Lucy wasn't the only one
excited about the day's event.
Snoopy and Woodstock
loved yard sales!

Woodstock chirped happily
and showed Snoopy an album.
Snoopy gave it a thumbs-down.

Snoopy and Woodstock
continued to look through
the items. They were looking for
the perfect thing.
But they couldn't seem to find it.

Just then, Snoopy spotted
an empty fishbowl.
Snoopy and Woodstock gasped.
This was it!
The perfect thing!

Snoopy and Woodstock imagined
they were deep-sea divers.
They couldn't believe all the
beautiful things they spotted
under the sea.
They even saw a mermaid!

But their daydream was quickly interrupted when they realized the mermaid was . . . Lucy!
"Can I help you?" she asked.
"I see you're interested in one of my precious artifacts."

Snoopy nodded and smiled.
He and Woodstock grabbed the
fishbowl and started to walk away.

"Not so fast!" Lucy yelled.
"This is a yard *sale*, not a yard-sale giveaway. Fifty cents, please!"

Snoopy didn't have any money,
but he *did* have a dog bone.
He tried to put it in the money tin.

"No dog bones," Lucy said.

Woodstock didn't have any money, either. But he did have a packet of birdseed!

"No birdseed, either!"
Lucy shouted.
"I need cold, hard cash!"
She took the fishbowl away
from them.

"Can you believe that dog?"
Lucy asked Linus.
"He expects quality merchandise
for free!"

"Well . . . not all economies exchanged money for merchandise," Linus said. "Some countries used to trade services for food and spices."

As Linus walked away,
Lucy thought for a moment.
You know, my brother may be a
blockhead, but sometimes he has
good ideas.

"Hey, Snoopy!" Lucy called.
"How about we trade services?
You two can do some chores
around the house, and
I'll give you the fishbowl.
Do we have a deal?"

Snoopy and Woodstock chatted for
a moment.
Snoopy then nodded in agreement
and shook hands with Lucy.

Lucy held up a list.
"You can start by painting the
fence," she began.
"Then you can cut the grass, do
the laundry, and fix the flat tire on
my bike."

Snoopy and Woodstock got right to work. Soon they were done painting the fence. But it wasn't exactly what Lucy had in mind. "This is a disaster!" she shouted.

Next, it was time for Snoopy and
Woodstock to mow the lawn.
They both had a difficult time
starting the mower.
Then the lawn mower took off on
its own!

Now it was time to do
Lucy's laundry.
Snoopy picked up a pile of blue
dresses and stuffed them in the
washing machine.

Then he dumped in a *lot* of
detergent.
Woodstock helped close the lid.

Lastly, it was time to fix
Lucy's flat tire.
Snoopy pumped the tire full of air.
A *lot* of air.
The tire suddenly popped, causing
the bike to fly through the air.

Just then, Lucy decided to check in
on Snoopy and Woodstock.
"What happened to the garden?"
she asked in disbelief.
"And is that my bike? And what's
that noise?"

"You blockhead!" she yelled.
"Forget about the list!
I'll make you a new deal.
Agree to *stop* doing chores for me,
and I'll give you the bowl, for *free*."

Woodstock and Snoopy thought
this was a great idea!
They shook hands with Lucy and
grabbed the fishbowl.
Then they headed back to
Snoopy's doghouse to go on
another exciting deep-sea
adventure!

Lucy sighed.
"Dogs and yard sales
definitely do *not* mix,"
she grumbled.